BIERCE: EASY TO READ

Easy To Read Series Vol. 3

**ARK   TUNDRA
PUBLISHING**

Bierce, Ambrose Gwinnett, 1842–1914
Bierce: Easy To Read / Ambrose Bierce
Completely revised and abridged text.

1. FICTION / Horror
2. LANGUAGE ARTS & DISCIPLINES / Reading Skills
3. STUDY AIDS / English Proficiency

ISBN: 978-91-88895-04-2

Cover Design and Layout: Ark Tundra

ARK TUNDRA
www.arktundra.com

This book is available at quantity discounts for
bulk purchases. For information, please e-mail us at
sales@arktundra.com, or call +44 (0) 186 55 22 572

The Damned Thing

I

By the light of a candle, which had been placed on one end of a table, a man was reading something written in a book. It was an old account book, and the writing was not very readable, for the man held it to the candle to get a better light on it. The shadow of the book would then darken a number of faces and figures; for besides the reader, eight other men were in the room. Seven of them sat silent against the walls, not very far from the table. The room was so small that by extending an arm any one of them could have touched the eighth man, who was laying on the table. He was partly covered by a sheet, and his arms were at his sides. He was dead.

No one spoke, and the man with the book was not reading out loud. All seemed to be waiting for something to happen; the dead man was the only one who did not expect anything. It was dark outside, and from out there all the noises of the night came in through a small window—the long howl of a coyote, the buzzing of insects, cries of owls; the drone of beetles, and all the other sounds. But no one in the company paid any attention to that; they were not very interested in matters that had no practical importance—it was obvious in every line of their faces. They were local men; farmers and woodworkers.

Only the man who was reading seemed to be different than the rest. One would have said that he looked worldly, but his clothing showed that he was from around the area.

His coat would hardly have met approval in a city, and his shoes were not the kind that one would see in a city either. His face was rather pleasing, with a slight hint of strictness. He looked like a person who was in authority. In fact, he was a coroner. It was in this capacity that he had the book, in which he was reading. It had been found among the dead man's possessions—in his cabin, where the investigation was now taking place.

When the coroner had finished reading he put the book into his breast pocket. At that moment the door opened and a young man entered. He, clearly, was not from the area: he was dressed as a man who dwelled in cities. His clothing was dusty, however, as from travel. He had, in fact, been riding hard to attend the investigation.

The coroner nodded, but no one else greeted him.

"We have waited for you," the coroner said. "It is necessary to finish this business tonight."

The young man smiled. "I am sorry to have kept you," he said. "I went away, not to avoid your calls, but to tell my newspaper what I am covering."

The coroner smiled.

"What you told your newspaper," he said, "is probably very different from what you will tell here under oath."

"That," replied the other, with obvious anxiety, "is as you choose. It was not written as news, because it is too incredible, but as fiction. It may pass as part of my testimony under oath."

"But you say it is incredible."

"That is nothing to you, sir, if I also swear that it is true."

The coroner was obviously not affected by the young man's anger. He was silent for a moment, and looked at the floor. The other men talked in whispers, but kept looking at the face of the corpse.

Soon the coroner lifted his eyes and said: "We will resume the investigation." The men removed their hats. The witness was sworn.

"What is your name?" the coroner asked.

"William Harker."

"Age?"

"Twenty-seven."

"You knew the deceased, Hugh Morgan?"

"Yes."

"You were with him when he died?"

"Near him."

"How did that happen—why were you present, I mean?"

"I was visiting him at his place to hunt and fish. But I was also going to study him and his solitary way of life. He seemed to be a good model for a character in fiction. I sometimes write stories."

"I sometimes read them."

"Thank you."

"Stories in general—not yours."

Some of the judges laughed. In such a dark environment humor shows high spirits. In between battles soldiers laugh easily, and a joke in the death chamber conquers by surprise.

"Tell the circumstances of this man's death," said the coroner. "You may use any notes that you please."

The witness understood and pulled up a manuscript from his breast pocket. He held it near the candle and began to read.

II

"It was still dark in the morning when we left the house. We were looking for quail, but we had only one dog. Morgan said that our best hunting ground was beyond a certain area that he pointed out. On the other side the ground was quite level and covered with wild oats.

"As we emerged from the forest, Morgan was just a few yards ahead of me. Suddenly, we heard a noise as of some animal beating around the bushes, which we could see were agitated.

"'We've started a deer,' I said. 'I wish we had brought a rifle.'

"Morgan said nothing as he closely watched the agitated forest. He had cocked both barrels of his gun, and was holding it, ready to fire. I thought he was a little excited, which surprised me, for he had a reputation of being unusually calm, even in moments of imminent danger.

"'Oh, come on!' I said. 'You are not going to kill a deer with quail-shot, are you?'

"He did not answer. I was struck by how pale his face was all of a sudden. Then I understood that we had serious business on hand, and my first guess was that we had 'jumped' a bear. I went to Morgan's side, and cocked my gun as I moved.

"The bushes were now quiet, and the sounds had stopped, but Morgan was as alert as before.

"'What is it? What the heck is it?' I asked.

"'That Damned Thing!' he replied, without turning his head. His voice was dry and unusual. He was trembling.

"I was about to say something, when I saw the wild oats near the place of the noise move. I can hardly describe it. It seemed as if it was moved by a wind, which not only bent it but pressed it down—crushed it so that it did not rise, and this movement was slowly coming toward us.

"Nothing that I had ever seen before had moved me so strangely as this miracle, but I did not feel any fear. I remember that once, as I looked out a window, I for a moment mistook a small tree for one of a group of larger trees farther away.

"It was about the same size as the others, but it seemed out of harmony with them, because of its shape. It was just a visual illusion but it alarmed me. We are so dependent on the well-ordered operation of the natural laws, that when they even deviate slightly from what we expect, we fear for our safety.

"So now the movement that did not seem to have a cause, and the slow approach of it toward us was unsettling. My companion was actually frightened, and I could not believe it when he suddenly threw his gun to his shoulder and fired both barrels at the grass!

"Before the gun smoke had cleared away, I heard a loud cry—like that of a wild animal—and, throwing his gun to the ground, Morgan ran away from the spot. At the same time I was violently thrown to the ground by the impact of something I could not see in the smoke— a soft, heavy something that hit me with great force.

"Before I could get back on my feet and get my gun, I heard Morgan cry out as if in mortal agony. I heard such savage sounds as one hears from fighting dogs. Terrified, I struggled to my feet and looked in the direction of Morgan's flight—may heaven in mercy spare me from another sight like that!

"Less than thirty yards away was my friend, down on one knee, his head thrown back, his long hair in disorder, and his body in violent movement from side to side.

"His right arm was lifted and the hand seemed to be missing—at least I could not see it. The other arm was invisible. At times, I could see only a part of his body; it was as if he had been partly blotted out—there is no other way of putting it—then a shift of his position would bring it all into view again.

"All this occurred within only a few seconds, but in that time Morgan looked like a wrestler beaten by superior weight and strength. I only ever saw him, and not always distinctly.

"During the entire incident his shouts were heard, as if through a barrage of sounds of rage as I had never heard from a man or brute!

"For a moment I could not move. Then I threw down my gun and ran to my friend's help. I had a vague belief that he was suffering from a fit or some form of convulsion. Before I could reach him, he was down and quiet. All sounds had stopped, but now I saw the same strange movement of the wild oats moving from the trampled area toward the forest. It was only when it had reached the wood that I could withdraw my eyes and look at my friend. He was dead."

III

The coroner rose from his seat and stood beside the dead man. He pulled away the sheet and exposed the entire naked body. It was yellowish, but had bluish-black marks, obviously caused by bruises. The chest and sides looked as if they had been beaten with a club. There were cuts; the skin was torn in strips and shreds.

Moving to the end of the table, the coroner untied a handkerchief that had been tied around the head. When it was drawn away it exposed what had been the throat.

Some of the jurors who had risen to get a better look turned their faces away in shock. Witness Harker leaned out of the open window, faint and sick.

As he dropped the handkerchief upon the dead man's neck, the coroner fetched one garment after another from a pile of clothing. He held each up for inspection. All were torn, and stiff with blood. The jurors did not take a closer look.

They seemed rather uninterested. Actually they had seen all this before; the only thing that was new to them was Harker's testimony.

"Gentlemen," the coroner said, "we have no more evidence, I think. Your duty has already been explained to you. If there is nothing you wish to ask, you may go outside and consider your verdict."

The foreman rose—a tall, bearded man of sixty.

"I would like to ask one question, Mr. Coroner," he said. "What mental asylum did your last witness escape from?"

"Mr. Harker," said the coroner, calmly, "from what mental asylum did you last escape?"

Harker's face turned red again, but he said nothing, and the seven jurors rose and left the cabin.

"If you are done insulting me, sir," said Harker, as soon as he and the coroner were alone with the dead man, "I suppose I am free to go?"

"Yes."

Harker was about to leave, but paused, with his hand on the door latch. The habit of his profession was strong in him—stronger than his self-respect.

He turned around and said:

"The book that you have there—I recognize it as Morgan's diary. You seem quite interested in it; you did read in it as I was testifying. May I see it? The public would like—"

"The book does not matter," replied the coroner and slipped it into his coat pocket; "all the entries in it were made before the writer's death."

As Harker left the house, the jury entered again and stood around the table on which the corpse showed a sharp outline under the sheet. The foreman seated himself near the candle, took a pencil and a scrap of paper, and wrote the following verdict, which all signed:

"We, the jury, do find that the corpse came to its death at the hands of a mountain lion, but some of us think it had fits."

IV

There are certain interesting entries in the diary of the late Hugh Morgan, which may have scientific value as suggestions. At the investigation of his body, the book was not used as evidence. Perhaps the coroner did not want to confuse the jury. It can't be determined when the first entry was exactly made because the upper part of the leaf is torn away. What remains of the entry tells the following:

" . . . would run in a half circle, his head always turned toward the center and then he would stand still, barking angrily. Finally he ran away as fast as he could. At first I thought that he had gone mad, but I found no other explanation than that he was afraid of punishment.

"Can a dog see with his nose? Do odors impress some foul center with images of the thing emitting them?

"September 2.—As I looked at the stars last night, I saw them disappear one after another—from left to right. Each was darkened for just a moment, and only a few at the same time, but along the entire length, all that were within my view were blotted out.

"It was as if something had passed along between me and them; but I could not see it. Ugh! I don't like this . . ." Several weeks' entries are missing, three leaves have been torn from the book.

"September 27.—It has been here again—I find traces of it every day. Last night I sat watching in the same cover again, gun in hand, double-charged. In the morning the fresh footprints were there, just as before. I swear that I did not sleep—indeed, I hardly sleep at all. It is terrible! If these experiences are real, I will go mad; if they are just a fantasy, then I am mad already.

"October 3.—I will not go—it will not drive me away. No, this is *my* house, *my* land. God hates a coward . . .

"October 5.—I can stand it no longer; I have invited Harker to stay a few weeks with me—he is levelheaded. I can judge from his manner if he thinks I am mad.

"October 7.—I have the solution to the problem; it came to me last night—suddenly, as if by revelation. How simple—how terribly simple!

"There are sounds that we cannot hear. There are notes that don't strike a chord in that imperfect instrument, the human ear. They are too high or too grave. I have observed a flock of blackbirds occupying an entire treetop—all in full song. Suddenly,—at the same instant—all spring into the air and fly away. How? They could not all see one another. At no point could a leader have been visible to all.

"There must have been a signal of command, high and shrill above the noise, but I could not hear it. I have also seen the same flight when all were silent, not only among blackbirds, but other birds—quail, for example, widely separated by bushes—even on the opposite sides of a hill.

"Seamen know that a school of whales sporting on the surface of the ocean, miles apart, will sometimes dive at the same time—all gone out of sight in a moment. The signal has been sounded—too grave for the ear of the sailor—who nevertheless feels its vibrations in the ship as the stones of a cathedral are stirred by the bass of the organ.

"As with sounds, so with colors. At each end of the solar spectrum, the chemist can detect the presence of certain rays. They represent colors, which we are unable to see. The human eye is an imperfect instrument; I am not mad; there are colors that we cannot see.

"And, God help me! the Damned Thing is of such a color!"

Present At A Hanging

An old man named Daniel Baker was suspected of having murdered a peddler who had been permitted to stay the night at his house. This was in 1853, when peddling was more common than it is now, and was a dangerous occupation. The peddler crossed the country on lonely roads, and relied on the hospitality of the country people. This brought him into contact with strange characters, some of whom were not altogether honorable in how they made a living, murder being an acceptable means to that end. Sometimes it happened that a peddler would be traced to the lonely house of some rough character and never could be traced beyond. That is the way it was in the case of "old man Baker," as he was called.

A peddler came to his house and never went away — that is all that anybody knew.

Seven years later the Reverend Mr. Cummings, a well-known Baptist minister, was driving by Baker's farm one night. It was not very dark as there was moonlight.

Mr. Cummings, who was always a cheerful person, was whistling a tune, which he would occasionally interrupt to speak to his horse. As he came to a little bridge he saw the figure of a man standing upon it.

The man had something strapped on his back and carried a heavy stick—obviously a travelling peddler. He looked like a sleepwalker. Mr. Cummings strapped his horse when he arrived in front of him, gave him a pleasant greeting and invited him to a seat in the vehicle—"if you are going my way," he added. The man raised his head and looked him in the face, but neither answered nor made any further movement. The minister repeated his invitation. At this the man threw his right hand forward and pointed downward as he stood on the edge of the bridge.

Mr. Cummings looked past him but saw nothing unusual and withdrew his eyes to address the man again. He had disappeared. At the same moment the horse gave a snort of terror and started to run away. Before he had regained control of the animal, the minister was at the top of the hill a hundred yards away. He looked back and saw the man again, at the same place as when he had first observed him. Then, for the first time, he was conscious of a sense of the supernatural and drove home as rapidly as his willing horse would go.

As he arrived home, he told his family about his adventure, and early the next morning he returned to the spot together with two neighbors. They found old man Baker hanging by the neck from one of the beams of the bridge, just beneath the spot where the man had stood.

A thick coating of dust covered the floor of the bridge, but the only footprints were those of Mr. Cummings' horse.

As the men took down the body, they disturbed the loose earth of the slope below. Nearly uncovered by the action of water and frost, there were human bones revealed down there. They were identified as those of the lost peddler. At the double inquest, they found that Daniel Baker died by his own hand while suffering from temporary insanity, and that Samuel Morritz was murdered by some person or persons that were not known to the jury.

A Cold Greeting

This is a story told by the late Benson Foley of San Francisco:

"In the summer of 1881 I met a man named James H. Conway. He was visiting San Francisco for his health, and brought me a letter of introduction from Mr. Lawrence Barting. I had known Barting as a captain during the civil war. He had settled in Franklin at its end, and became somewhat famous as a lawyer. Barting had always struck me as an honorable man, and the friendship which he expressed in his letter for Mr. Conway was sufficient evidence to me that Conway was worthy of my esteem. At dinner one day, Conway told me that it had been agreed between him and Barting that the one who died first should communicate with the other from beyond the grave. Just how, they had left to be decided by the deceased.

"A few weeks after this conversation, I met him one day as he was slowly walking down Montgomery street in deep thought.

"He greeted me coldly with a movement of the head and passed on, leaving me with my hand extended. The next day I met him again in the office of the Palace Hotel, and as he was about to repeat the act of the day before, I stopped him in a doorway with a friendly salutation. I bluntly demanded an explanation for his strange behavior. He hesitated for a moment; then he looked me in the eye and said: 'I do not think, Mr. Foley, that I any longer have a claim to your friendship, since Mr. Barting appears to have withdrawn his own from me. If he has not already informed you, he will probably do so.'

"'But,' I replied, 'I have not heard from Mr. Barting.'

"'Heard from him!' he repeated in surprise. 'Why, he is here. I met him yesterday just before meeting you. I gave you exactly the same greeting that he gave me. I met him again barely an hour ago, and his manner was exactly the same: he bowed and passed on. I will not forget your friendliness to me. Good morning, or—farewell.'

"All this seemed to me very considerate on the part of Mr. Conway.

"As dramatic situations and effects are not part of my purpose, I will explain that Mr. Barting was dead.

"He had died in Nashville four days before this conversation. Calling on Mr. Conway, I told him of our friend's death and showed him the obituary. He was very affected in such a way that did not make me question his sincerity."

"'It seems incredible,' he said. 'I guess I have mistaken another man for Barting, and that man's cold greeting was just a stranger's greeting of my own. In fact, I remember that he lacked Barting's mustache.'

"It was without doubt another man,' I agreed; and the subject was never mentioned again between us. But in my pocket I had a photograph of Barting, which had been enclosed in the letter from his widow. It had been taken a week before his death, and was without a mustache."

A Wireless Message

In the summer of 1896, Mr. William Holt, a wealthy industrialist of Chicago, was living in a little town of central New York. Mr. Holt had "trouble with his wife," whom he had left a year before.

Whether the trouble was anything serious, he is probably the only living person that knows: he is not the type of man who seeks to unburden his soul to other people. But he has told at least one person about the incident that we are about to recount. He is now living in Europe.

One evening he had left the house of his brother for a stroll in the country. It may be assumed that his mind was occupied with thoughts of his marital problems and the sad changes that they had on his life.

Whatever his thoughts may have been, he was so possessed by them that he forgot the time and did not know where he was going. He only knew that he had gone far beyond the town limit and was crossing a lonely road that did not look like the one that he had left behind. In brief, he was lost.

Realizing his bad luck, he smiled. Central New York was not a dangerous place in those days, and one did not remain lost in it very long. He turned around and went back the way that he had come. Before he had gone far, he saw that the landscape was more distinct and brighter. Everything was covered with a red glow, in which he saw his shadow projected in the road before him.

"The moon is rising," he said to himself. Then he remembered that it was about the time of the new moon. He stopped and looked around, trying to find the source of the bright light. At the same time his shadow turned and lay along the road in front of him as before. The light still came from behind him. That was surprising; he could not understand it. He turned again, and again, facing every point of the horizon. The shadow was always in front of him—the light always behind him, an awful red.

Holt was astonished, but he seems to have retained a certain curiosity. To test the intensity of the light, whose cause he could not determine, he took out his watch to see if he could make out the figures on the dial. They were visible, and the hands indicated the hour of eleven o'clock and twenty-five minutes.

At that moment the strange light suddenly flared to an intense splendor, extinguishing the stars in the sky and throwing the big shadow of himself across the landscape.

In that brilliance he saw in the air the elevated figure of his wife, dressed in her night-gown and holding to her breast his child. Her eyes were fixed upon his with an expression that was not of this life.

The flare was brief, followed by darkness. But the ghost was still visible, white and motionless. Then it vanished, like an image on the retina after the closing of the eyes. The strangeness of the ghost was that it showed only the upper half of the woman's figure and nothing below the waist.

The sudden darkness was not total, for slowly all objects of his surroundings became visible again.

In the dawn, Holt found himself entering the village from the opposite end. He soon arrived at the house of his brother, who hardly recognized him. He was wild-eyed, haggard, and gray as a rat. Ramblingly, he told him of his night's experience.

"Go to bed, my poor fellow," his brother said, "and—wait. We will hear more of this."

An hour later the predestined telegram came. Holt's house had been destroyed by fire. The flames had cut off his wife's escape, as she had appeared at a window with her child in her arms.

There she had stood, motionless, confused. Just as the firemen had arrived with a ladder, the floor had given way, and she was seen no more.

The moment of this culminating horror was eleven o'clock and twenty-five minutes, standard time.

An Arrest

Having murdered his brother-in-law, Orrin Brower was a fugitive from justice. He had escaped from the county jail by knocking down his jailer, robbing him of his keys and, opening the outer door, walking out into the night. Because the jailer was unarmed, Brower got no weapon with which to defend his new freedom. As soon as he was out of the town, he entered a forest; this was many years ago, when that region was wilder than it is now.

The night was dark, and neither the moon nor stars were visible. As Brower had never been in the area, it did not take long until he was lost. He could not have said if he were getting farther away from the town or going back to it. He knew that in either case a gang of citizens with a pack of dogs would soon be on his track and his chance of escape was very slim.

Suddenly he emerged from the forest into an old road, and before him he saw the figure of a man. It was too late to retreat: the fugitive felt that at the first turnaround he would be shot.

The two stood there like trees, Brower nearly suffocated by the pounding of his own heart; the other—the emotions of the other are not recorded.

A moment later—it may have been an hour—the moon came out and the hunted man saw the figure of the man lift an arm and point toward and beyond him. He understood. He turned his back and walked away in the direction indicated, neither looking to the right nor to the left.

Brower was the bravest criminal to ever be hanged; that was shown by the conditions of awful personal danger in which he had coolly killed his brother-in-law. It is needless to relate them here; they came out at his trial, and the revelation of his calmness in confronting them almost saved his neck. But what would you have?—when a brave man is beaten, he submits.

And so they followed their journey to jail along the old road through the woods. Brower only once turned his head: Just once did he look back, when he was in a deep shadow and he knew that the other was in the moonlight.

His captor was Burton Duff, the jailer, as white as death and his brow bore the mark of the iron bar that Bower had used to knock him out.

Eventually they reached the town, which was deserted. Only the women and children remained, and they were off the streets. Brower walked straight toward the jail. He walked straight up to the main entrance, pushed open the heavy iron door, entered, and found himself in the presence of half a dozen armed men. Then he turned. Nobody else entered.

On a table in the corridor lay the dead body of Burton Duff.

A Man With Two Lives

Here is the strange story of David William Duck, as told by himself. Duck is an old man living in Aurora, Illinois, where he is liked by everyone. He is commonly known, however, as "Dead Duck."

"In the autumn of 1866 I was a private soldier of the Eighteenth Infantry. My company was one of those stationed at Fort Phil Kearney, commanded by Colonel Carrington. The country is more or less familiar with the history of that garrison, particularly with the slaughter by the Sioux of eighty-one men and officers. Not one escaped. When that occurred, I was trying to make my way with important dispatches to Fort C. F. Smith, on the Big Horn. As the country was full with hostile enemies, I traveled by night and concealed myself before daybreak.

"For my second place of hiding, I chose what seemed like a narrow canon leading through a range of hills. It had many large rocks, detached from the slopes. Behind one of these I made my bed for the day, and soon fell asleep.

"It seemed as if I had hardly closed my eyes when I was awakened by a bullet striking the boulder just above my body. A band of enemies had followed me and had me nearly surrounded. The shot had been fired by a fellow who had caught sight of me from the hillside above. The smoke of his rifle gave him away, and I was on my feet before he was rolling down the declivity. Then I ran dodging a storm of bullets from invisible enemies. The rascals did not pursue me, which I thought was strange, for they must have known that they only dealt with one man. The reason for their inaction soon became clear. I had not gone a hundred yards before I reached the limit of my run—the end of the ravine, which I had mistaken for a canon. It ended in a breast of rock that was nearly vertical. I was caught in that dead end like a bear in a cage. Hunting me was needless; they only had to wait.

"They waited. For two days and two nights, crouching behind a rock, with the cliff at my back, I suffered agonies of thirst, and had no hopes of escape. I fought the fellows from a distance as I fired at the smoke of their rifles, as they did at that of mine. I did not dare to close my eyes at night, and the lack of sleep was torture. I remember the morning of the third day, which I knew was to be my last. I remember that in my desperation I jumped out into the open and began firing my rifle without seeing anybody to fire at. And I remember no more of that fight.

"The next thing that I remember was pulling myself out of a river at nightfall. I did not have a rag of clothing and did not know where I was, but I traveled all night toward the north. At daybreak I found myself at Fort C. F. Smith, but without my dispatches. The first man that I met was a sergeant named William Briscoe, whom I knew very well. You can imagine his surprise at seeing me in that condition, and my own, when he asked me who the heck I was.

"'Dave Duck,' I answered; 'who would I be?'

"He stared like an owl.

"'You do look like it,' he said, and I saw that he drew a little away from me. 'What's up?' he added.

"I told him what had happened to me the day before. He listened to me, and said:

"'My dear fellow, if you are Dave Duck I should inform you that I buried you two months ago. I was out with a small scouting party and found your body, full of bullet-holes and newly scalped—a little mutilated, too, I am sorry to say—right where you say you made your fight. Come to my tent and I'll show you your clothing and some letters that I took from your corpse.'

"He did what he had promised. He showed me the clothing, which I then put on, and the letters, which I put into my pocket. Then he took me to the commander, who heard my story and ordered Briscoe to take me to the prison. On the way I said:

"'Bill Briscoe, did you really bury the dead body that you found in these clothes?'

"'Sure,' he answered—'just as I told you. It was Dave Duck, all right; most of us knew him. And now, you damned impostor, you'd better tell me who you are.'

"'I would like to know that too,' I said.

"A week later, I escaped from the prison and got out of the country as fast as I could. I have been back twice, looking for that fateful spot in the hills, but was unable to find it."

A Baffled Ambuscade

Connecting Readyville and Woodbury was a turnpike that was at least ten miles long. Readyville was an outpost of the Federal army; Woodbury was the same to the Confederate army. For months after the big battle at Stone River these outposts were in constant quarrel. Most of the trouble occurred on the turnpike.

One night, a troop of Federal horses led by Major Seidel, a skillful officer, moved out from Readyville on a dangerous mission that had to be kept secret.

Passing the infantry pickets, they soon approached two cavalry videttes staring into the darkness ahead. There should have been three.

"Where is your other man?" said the major. "I ordered Dunning to be here tonight."

"He rode ahead, sir," the man replied. "Then we heard some firing, but it was a long way to the front."

"It was against orders and against sense for Dunning to do that," said the officer, obviously angry.

"Why did he ride ahead?"

"Don't know, sir; he seemed restless. Guess he was scared."

When the two men had been taken into the troop, it continued its journey. Talking was forbidden; arms and belongings were not allowed to make a sound if they rattled. Only the horses' trampling could be heard and they moved slowly in order to have as little as possible of that. It was past midnight and pretty dark, although the moon shone somewhere behind the clouds.

About three miles along the path, they approached a forest. The major told the troop to stop, and, evidently a bit scared himself, he rode ahead alone to take a look. He was followed, however, by his assistant and three troopers, who remained behind and saw all that occurred.

After riding about a hundred yards toward the forest, the major suddenly stopped his horse and sat in the saddle without moving. Near the side of the road, in a little open space, stood the figure of a man, barely visible, and as motionless as the major. The major's first feeling was that of satisfaction in having left his group behind. Because if this were an enemy, he would have been shot right away.

The troop had not been detected yet. A dark object could be seen at the man's feet. The officer could not make out what it was. With the instinct of the true soldier, he drew his sword. The man on foot still did not move. The situation was tense and a bit dramatic. Suddenly the moon burst through the clouds and the horseman saw the footman clearly in the white light. It was Trooper Dunning, unarmed and bareheaded. The object at his feet was a dead horse, and across the animal's neck lay a dead man, face upward in the moonlight.

"Dunning had the fight of his life," thought the major, and was about to ride ahead. Dunning raised his hand, signaling him back with a gesture of warning. Then he lowered his arm and pointed to the place where the road led into the forest.

The major understood, turned his horse and rode back to the group that had followed him.

"Dunning is just ahead there," he said to the captain of his leading company. "He has killed this man and will have something to report."

They waited patiently, swords drawn, but Dunning did not come. In an hour the day broke and they all moved forward, its commander not satisfied with his faith in Private Dunning.

The expedition had failed, but there remained something to be done. In the little open space off the road they found the dead horse. Across animal's neck, face upward, a bullet in the brain, lay the body of Trooper Dunning, stiff as a statue, dead for hours.

An examination showed evidence that within half an hour the forest had been occupied by a force of Confederate infantry—an ambush.

Two Military Executions

In the spring of the year 1862, General Buell's big army lay in camp, preparing themselves for the campaign, which resulted in the victory at Shiloh. It was an untrained army, although some of it had seen hard action in the mountains of Western Virginia.

The war had just begun and created a new industry, which was not entirely understood by people at the time. Most important in all of it was subordination. To a person filled with the misbelief that all men are born equal, submission to authority is not an easy task, and the American volunteer in his "green and salad days" is among the worst there is.

And that is how it happened that one of Buell's men, Private Greene, committed the indiscretion of punching his officer. Later in the war he would not have done that. Like Sir Andrew Aguecheek, he would have "seen him damned" first. But he was denied the opportunity to regain his status and was arrested on complaint of the officer, tried by court-martial and sentenced to death.

"You might have beat me and left it at that," he said to the complaining witness; "that is what you used to do at school, when you were plain Will Dudley and I was as good as you. Nobody saw me punch you."

"Private Greene, I guess you are right about that," the lieutenant said. "Will you forgive me? That is what I came to see you about."

There was no reply, and an officer explained that the time for the interview was over. The next morning, in the presence of the whole brigade, Private Greene was shot to death by a squad of his own comrades. Lieutenant Dudley turned his back and muttered a prayer for mercy, in which he himself was included.

A few weeks later, as Buell's division was being ferried over a River to assist Grant's beaten army, a stormy night was coming on. The division moved through the wreck of the battleground in the direction of the enemy, who had withdrawn a little. But the darkness was total, with the thunder lightening. It did not cease for a moment, and even when it did not roar, the moans of the wounded were heard, as the men stumbled upon them in the darkness. The dead were there, too — many of them. In the gray of the morning, when the division had paused to line up, word was passed along to call the roll.

The first sergeant of Dudley's company stepped to the front and named the men in alphabetical order. He had no written note, but a good memory.

The men answered to their names as he ran down the alphabet to G.

"Gorham."

"Here!"

"Grayrock."

"Here!"

The sergeant's good memory was affected by habit:

"Greene."

"Here!"

The response was clear, distinct, and unmistakable!

A sudden agitation of the entire company front, as if hit by an electric shock, showed how startling the incident was. The sergeant turned pale.

The captain stepped quickly to his side and said:

"Call that name again."

Apparently the Society for Psychical Research is not first in the field of curiosity when it comes to the Unknown.

"Bennett Greene."

"Here!"

All faces turned in the direction of the familiar voice. The two men, between whom Greene had commonly stood before, looked at each other.

"One more time," commanded the investigator, and one more time—a little tremulously—the name of the dead man:

"Bennett Story Greene."

"Here!"

At that instant a rifle-shot was heard beyond the battle line. It was followed by the hiss of an approaching bullet, which punctuated as with a full stop the captain's exclamation, "What the devil does it mean?"

Lieutenant Dudley pushed through the ranks.

"This is what it means" he said, as he threw open his coat and displayed a broadening stain of red on his breast. His knees gave way; he fell down and was dead.

Later the regiment was ordered to relieve the overfilled front. Though a misplay in the game of battle was not again under fire. Nor did Bennett Greene, expert in military executions, ever again signify his presence at one.

The Isle Of Pines

For many years there lived an old man named Herman Deluse near the town of Gallipolis, Ohio. Very little was known of his life, for he never spoke of it himself. It was commonly believed that he had been a pirate—if nothing else because of his collection of boarding pikes, cutlasses, and ancient flintlock pistols.

He lived alone in a small house of four rooms that was falling apart and was never repaired more than necessary. It stood on an elevation in the middle of a large field, which was barely cultivated. It was his only visible property, but it could hardly have made him a living. He always seemed to have money, and paid for all his purchases in cash, never going to the same store more than three times. People thought that it was an attempt to conceal the fact that he had much more money than believed.

That he had hoards of gold buried somewhere around his decrepit house was not to be doubted by anyone who knew local traditions and had their wits about them. On the ninth of November, 1867, the old man died.

Or at least his dead body was discovered on the tenth, and doctors testified that death had occurred about twenty-four hours before—but how, they were unable to say. The autopsy showed every organ to be healthy, with no indication of sickness or violence.

According to them, death must have taken place around midday, but the body was found in bed. The verdict of the coroner's jury was that he "came to his death by a visitation of God." The body was buried and the public administrator took charge of the estate.

A rigorous search revealed nothing more than what was already known about the dead man. The administrator locked up the house until it would be sold by law.

The night of November 20 was lively. A wind stormed across the country. Great trees were torn from the earth and hurled across the roads. The region had never experienced such a wild night, but toward morning the storm had blown off and the day dawned bright and clear.

At about eight o'clock, the Reverend Henry Galbraith, a highly esteemed Lutheran minister, arrived on foot at his house. Mr. Galbraith had been in Cincinnati for a month.

He had come up the river in a steamboat and had set out on horse the previous evening. The storm had delayed him over night, and in the morning the fallen trees had forced him to abandon his horse and continue his journey on foot.

"But where did you pass the night?" his wife asked, after he had briefly told her his adventure.

"With old Deluse at the 'Isle of Pines,'" was his laughing reply; "and I sure had a dark time there. He did not object to my staying there, but he did not say a single word."

Luckily Mr. Robert Mosely Maren, a lawyer of Columbus, was present at this conversation. Noting, but not sharing, the astonishment caused by Mr. Galbraith's answer, this Mr. Maren calmly asked: "Why did you go there?"

This is Mr. Maren's version of Mr. Galbraith's reply:

"I saw a light in the house, and drove in at the gate and put up my horse in the old rail stable, where it is now. I then knocked on the door, and as I got no invitation, I went in without one. The room was dark, but I had matches and lit a candle.

"I tried to enter the room, but the door was locked, and although I heard the old man's footsteps in there, he did not answer my calls.

"There was no fire on the hearth, so I made one and laid down before it, ready to go to sleep. Soon the door that I had tried opened and the old man came in, carrying a candle. I spoke to him and apologized for my intrusion, but he took no notice of me. He seemed to be searching for something, though his eyes did not move in their sockets. I wonder if he ever walks in his sleep. He walked around the room, and went out the same way he had come in. He came back two more times into the room before I slept, and acted the same way, and left again. In between these visits I heard him walking around the house. His footsteps were audible in the quiet moments of the storm. When I awoke in the morning he had already gone out."

Mr. Maren asked some further questions, but was unable to restrain the family's tongues. The story of Deluse's death and burial came out, to the minister's astonishment.

"The explanation of your adventure is very simple," said Mr. Maren. "I don't believe old Deluse walks in his sleep—not in his present one; but you evidently dream in yours."

And with this view of the matter Mr. Galbraith reluctantly agreed.

Nevertheless, the next night these two gentlemen and the son of the minister found themselves in front of the old Deluse house. There appeared a light in one window, then in another. The three men went to the door. Just as they reached it, there came the most terrible sounds from inside—a clash of weapons, steel against steel, sharp explosions as of firearms, shrieks of women, groans and the curses of men in combat!

The investigators stood a moment, frightened. Then Mr. Galbraith tried the door. It was locked. But the minister was a man of courage and of great strength. He rushed against the door, striking it with his right shoulder, and burst it from the frame with a loud crash. In a moment the three were inside. Darkness and silence! The only sound was the beating of their hearts.

Mr. Maren had matches and a candle. With some difficulty he made a light, and they went on to explore the place, going from room to room.

Everything was just as it had been left by the sheriff; nothing had been disturbed. A light coating of dust was everywhere.

A back door was partly open, and their first thought was that what had caused the noises had escaped. The door was opened, and the light of the candle shone through upon the ground.

The storm of the night before had brought a light fall of snow; there were no footprints in the white surface. They closed the door and entered the last room. Here the candle in Mr. Maren's hand was suddenly extinguished, following the sound of a heavy fall. When the candle had been relighted, young Mr. Galbraith was seen laying on the floor. He was dead.

In one hand he grasped a heavy sack of coins, which later all turned out to be of old Spanish origin. Directly over the body, a board had been torn from the wall, and it was evident that the bag had been taken from the cavity.

There was another investigation: another autopsy failed to reveal a cause of death. Another verdict of "the visitation of God" left it up to everyone to form their own conclusion as to what had happened. Mr. Maren stated that the young man had died of excitement.

A Fruitless Assignment

Henry Saylor, who was killed in a quarrel with Antonio Finch, was a reporter at the Cincinnati Newspaper. In the year 1859, a vacant house in Cincinnati became the center of excitement because of the strange things said to be going on there at night. According to many reputable residents in the area, there was no other explanation than that the house was haunted. Unfamiliar figures were seen on the sidewalk, coming in and out of the place. No one could say just where they appeared on the lawn on their way to the front door, nor at what point they disappeared as they came out. And while each spectator was certain about these matters, no one agreed.

Some of the bolder ones dared to stand on the doorsteps to stop them on several evenings, or at least get a better look at them.

These courageous men were unable to open the door by their united strength, and were always injured as they were pushed from the steps by something invisible. Afterward the door immediately opened on its own.

The house was known as the Roscoe house. A family of that name had lived there for some years, and then, one by one, disappeared. The last to leave was an old woman. There were stories of foul play and murders, but none were ever proven.

One day during all this excitement, Saylor presented himself at the office of the Cincinnati newspaper. He received a note from the city editor, which read as follows: "Go and spend the night alone in the haunted house in Vine Street, and if anything interesting occurs, write two columns." Saylor obeyed his superior; he could not afford to lose his position on the paper.

He gained access to the house through a rear window before dark, walked through the deserted rooms, dusty and desolate, and seated himself at last in the salon on a sofa as night came on.

Before it was dark, the crowd had gathered in the street, silent and expectant. Here and there someone uttered disbelief. No one knew that Saylor was inside. He was afraid to turn on a light; the windows would have made his presence known and could have subjected him to insult, or even to injury. Moreover, he was too careful to do anything to change the conditions under which the strange things were said to occur.

It was now dark outside, but light from the street lit up part of the room that he was in. He had opened every door inside the house, but all the outer ones were locked. Sudden shouts from the crowd caused him to jump to the window and look out. He saw the figure of a man move rapidly across the lawn toward the building — saw it go up the steps; then he lost sight of it as it slipped behind a wall. There was a noise as of the opening and closing of the hall door. He heard quick footsteps — heard them go upstairs — heard them on the uncarpeted floor of the chamber overhead.

Saylor drew his pistol, and going upstairs entered the chamber, dimly lit from the street. No one was there. He heard footsteps in the next room and entered that. It was dark and silent. His foot struck against an object on the floor; he knelt down and passed his hand over it. It was a human head — that of a woman. Lifting it by the hair, he returned to the half-lit room below, carried it near the window and examined it. As he did this, he was not aware of the opening and closing of the outer door, of footsteps sounding all around him.

He raised his eyes from the terrible object and found himself surrounded by a crowd of men and women that were only dimly seen; the room was full with them. He thought the people had broken in.

"Ladies and gentlemen," he said, coolly, "you see me under suspicious circumstances, but" — his voice was drowned by laughter — the type of laughter that is heard in mental asylums. The persons around him pointed at the object in his hand, and their cheerfulness increased as he dropped it and it rolled among their feet. They danced around it with terrible motions. They struck it with their feet, moving it from wall to wall; pushed one another in their struggles to kick it; cursed and sang songs as the head went around the room as if trying to escape. At last it shot out of the door into the hall, and all rushed after it. That moment the door closed. Saylor was alone, in dead silence.

He put away his pistol, which he had held in his hand the whole time, and looked out the window. The street was deserted. He left the house and walked to the newspaper's office. The city editor was still in his office — asleep. Saylor woke him up and said: "I have been at the haunted house."

The editor stared as if not wholly awake. "Good God!" he cried, "are you Saylor?"

"Yes — why?" The editor did not answer, but continued staring.

"I passed the night there–it seems," said Saylor.

"They say that things were unusually quiet out there," the editor said, toying with a paper-weight, "did anything happen?"

"No, Nothing."

A Vine On A House

About three miles from the little town of Norton, in Missouri, stands an old house that was last occupied by a family named Harding. Since 1886 no one has lived in it, nor is anyone likely to live in it again. An observer who does not know its history would not put it into the category of "haunted houses," but that is its reputation in the region. Its windows are without glass, its doorways without doors; there are holes in the roof, and the weatherboarding is gray. But these signs of the supernatural are partly concealed by the greenery of a vine that overruns the entire place.

This vine—no botanist has ever been able to name its species—has an important part in the story of the house.

The Harding family consisted of Robert Harding, his wife Matilda; Miss Julia Went, who was her sister, and two young children. Robert Harding was a quiet man who made no friends in the neighborhood. He was about forty years old, frugal and industrious, and made a living from the little farm, which is now overgrown with brushes. Their neighbors seemed to think that he and his sister-in-law were seen too often together—which was not entirely their fault, for at these times they did not challenge observation. The moral code of rural Missouri is strict and demanding.

Mrs. Harding was a gentle, sad-eyed woman, who was missing her left foot.

At some time in 1884 it became known that she had gone to visit her mother in Iowa. That was what her husband said when people asked. She never came back, and two years later, without selling his farm or anything that was his, Harding left the country with the rest of the family. Nobody knew where he went, and at that time nobody cared. Naturally, whatever was movable in the place soon disappeared and the deserted house became "haunted" in the manner of its kind.

One summer evening, years later, the Reverend J. Gruber, of Norton, and a Maysville attorney called Hyatt met on horseback in front of the Harding place.

As they had matters to discuss, they hitched their animals and sat on the porch of the house to talk. They joked about the reputation of the house, but soon forgot about it, and they talked of their business affairs until night came.

The evening was hot, the air still. Suddenly both men jumped from their seats in surprise: a long vine that dangled its branches from the edge of the porch above them was visibly agitated, shaking violently in every stem and leaf.

"We will have a storm," Hyatt shouted.

Gruber said nothing, but silently directed the other's attention to the greenery of the trees, which showed no movement. Even the tips of the branches against the clear sky did not move.

They quickly went down the steps and looked up at the vine, whose entire length was now visible. It continued in violent agitation, but they could not tell what disturbed it.

"Let us leave," the minister said.

And so they did. Forgetting that they had been traveling in opposite directions, they rode away together. They went to Norton, where they told their strange experience to several friends. The next evening, accompanied by two others, they were again on the porch of the Harding house, and again the strange phenomenon occurred: the vine was agitated while they scrutinized it from root to tip, and even their combined strength could not serve to still it. After an hour's observation they retreated, still without an idea as to what caused it. It did not take long to rouse the curiosity of the neighborhood.

Day and night did crowds gather at the Harding house, "looking for a sign." But no one saw it, even though testimonies were so credible that no one doubted the reality of the "manifestations."

One day it was proposed to dig up the vine, and after a good deal of debate this was done. Nothing was found but the root, but nothing could have been more strange!

About six feet from the trunk, which at the top of the ground had a diameter of several inches, it ran down into a crumbly earth. Then it divided into rootlets, fibers, and filaments. When freed from soil they showed a strange formation. In their doublings back upon themselves, they made a compact network, having in size and shape an amazing likeness to the human figure.

Head, trunk, and limbs were there; even the fingers and toes were clearly defined. Many claimed to see in the arrangement in the green mass the head of a grotesque suggestion of a face. The figure was horizontal; the smaller roots had begun to unite at the breast.

The similarity to the human form was flawed. At about ten inches from one of the knees, where the leg forms, it had doubled backward and inward upon their course of growth. The figure lacked the left foot.

There was but one inference—the obvious one, and in the excitement that followed, many courses of action were suggested. The matter was settled by the sheriff, who as the lawful custodian of the estate ordered the root to be placed back, and the hole filled with the earth that had been removed.

Later inquiry only brought one interesting fact to light: Mrs. Harding had never visited her relatives in Iowa, nor did they know that she was supposed to have done so.

Nothing is known about the whereabouts of Robert Harding and the rest of his family. The house retains its evil reputation, but the vine is as orderly as a nervous person could wish to sit under on a pleasant night, when the insects grate out their immemorial revelation and the distant whippoorwill signifies his notion of what ought to be done about it.

At Old Man Eckert's

Philip Eckert lived for many years in an old wooden house about three miles from the town of Marion, in Vermont. There must be quite a number of persons still alive who remember him, but not unkindly.

"Old Man Eckert," as he was called, was not very friendly and lived alone. As he was never known to speak of himself, nobody knew anything of his past, nor of his relatives, if he had any. Without being particularly revolting in manner or speech, he somehow managed to be immune to people's curiosity.

As far as I know, Mr. Eckert's reputation as a former assassin or a retired pirate had not reached any ear in Marion. He made his living by cultivating a small and not very fertile farm.

One day he disappeared and a long search by his neighbors failed to find him. Nor could they throw any light upon his whereabouts. Nothing indicated that he had planned to leave: all was as he had left it.

For a few weeks, it was the only subject that was talked about in that region; then "old man Eckert" became a village tale for the ear of the stranger. I do not know what happened to his property. The house was standing, still vacant and unfit, when I last heard of it, some twenty years later.

Of course it came to be known as "haunted," and the usual tales were told of moving lights, strange sounds, and weird sights. At one time, about five years after the disappearance, these stories became so common, that Marion's most serious citizens decided to investigate. They arranged for a night session on the premises, and the parties involved were John Holcomb, a pharmacist; Wilson Merle, a lawyer, and Andrus C. Palmer, the teacher of the public school.

They were to meet at Holcomb's house at eight o'clock in the evening and go together to the scene of their night watch.

Palmer did not keep the engagement, and after waiting for half an hour for him, the others went to the Eckert house without him. They seated themselves in the principal room, before a glowing fire, and waited for the events. They had agreed to speak as little as possible: They did not even discuss the absence of Palmer, which had occupied their minds on the way.

An hour had passed without incident when they heard the sound of a door open in the rear of the house, followed by footsteps in the next room. The watchers rose to their feet, but stayed put, and prepared for whatever might happen. A long silence followed—how long neither one could say. Then the door between the two rooms opened and a man entered.

It was Palmer. He was pale, as if from excitement. His manner, too, was strange: He did not respond to their salutations, nor did he look at them, but walked slowly across the room, opened the front door, and disappeared into the darkness.

It seems to have been the first thought of both men that Palmer was suffering from fright—that he had heard, or seen, or imagined something in the back room that had deprived him of his senses. Both of them ran after him through the open door. But neither they nor anyone else ever saw or heard of Andrus Palmer again!

This much was clear the next morning. During the session of Holcomb and Merle at the "haunted house," a new snow had fallen and covered the ground with several inches. In this snow, Palmer's trail from his lodging in the village to the back door of the Eckert house was visible.

But there it ended: from the front door, nothing led away but the tracks of the two men who swore that he preceded them.

Palmer's disappearance was as complete as that of "old man Eckert" himself—whom, indeed, the editor of the local paper somewhat graphically accused of having "reached out and pulled him in."

The Spook House

On the road leading north from Manchester to Booneville stood a wooden plantation house in 1862. The house was destroyed by fire in the following year—probably caused by some stragglers from the column of General George W. Morgan that was retreating when he was driven away. At the time of its destruction, it had been vacant for about five years. The fields around it were overgrown with brambles, the fences gone, and everything had fallen into ruin by neglect and pillage.

It was known as the "Spook House." No one in that region doubted that it was inhabited by evil spirits any more than he doubted what he was told on Sundays by the preacher. The opinion of its owner was not known; he and his family had disappeared one night and no trace of them had ever been found. They left everything—household goods, clothing, provisions, the horses in the stable, the cows in the field—all as it stood. Nothing was missing—except a man, a woman, three girls, a boy, and a baby. One night in June, two citizens of Frankfort, Colonel J. C. McArdle, a lawyer, and Judge Myron Veigh, of the State Militia, were driving from Booneville to Manchester.

Their business was so important that they decided to push on, despite the darkness and an approaching storm, which broke upon them just as they arrived by the "Spook House." The lightning was so relentless that they easily found their way into a shed, where they hitched their team.

They then went to the house and knocked on all the doors without getting any response. Assuming that this was because of the roar of the thunder, they pushed at one of the doors, which yielded. They entered and closed the door. That instant they were in darkness and silence. Not a gleam of the lightning's blaze entered the windows; not a whisper of the noise outside reached them there.

It was as if they had suddenly been stricken blind and deaf, and McArdle later said that for a moment he believed himself to have been killed by a stroke of lightning as he crossed the threshold. The rest of this adventure can as well be retold in his own words, from the Frankfort Newspaper of August sixth, 1876:

"When I had recovered from the effect of the transition from roar to silence, my first urge was to open the door again, which I had closed. By stepping out into the storm I wanted to make sure that I had not been deprived of sight and hearing.

"I turned the doorknob and pulled open the door. It led into another room! This room was bathed with a greenish light, I could not tell where it came from. It made everything clearly visible, though nothing was defined. Everything, I say—but in truth the only objects within the stone walls of that room were human corpses.

"There were eight or ten of them—I did not really count them. They were of different ages, or sizes, from infancy up, and of both sexes. All were flat on the floor, except one, a young woman apparently, who sat up with her back against the wall. A baby was grasped in the arms of another woman. A half-grown boy lay face down across the legs of a full-bearded man.

"One or two were nearly naked, and the hand of a young girl held the piece of a gown, which she had torn open at the breast. The bodies were in various stages of decay, all greatly shrunken in face and figure. Some were little more than skeletons.

"While I was dazed with horror by this ghastly sight and still holding open the door, my attention was distracted from the scene and concerned itself with small details. Perhaps my mind sought relief in things, which would relax its tension. Among other things, I saw that the door that I was holding open was of heavy iron plates.

"Three strong bolts protruded from the beveled edge. I turned the knob and they retracted even with the edge; when I released it, they shot out. It was a spring lock. On the inside there was no knob, nor any kind of projection—a smooth surface of iron.

"While noting these things I felt myself thrust aside, and Judge Veigh, whom I in the intensity of my feelings had forgotten, pushed by me into the room. 'For God's sake,' I cried, 'do not go in there! Let us get out of this dreadful place!'

"He did not pay attention to my pleas, but walked to the center of the room, knelt beside one of the bodies for a closer look, and tenderly raised its blackened and shriveled head in his hands.

"A strong odor came through the doorway, completely overpowering me. My senses reeled. I felt myself falling, and as I clutched at the edge of the door for support, I pushed it shut with a sharp click!

"I remember nothing after that: six weeks later I came to my senses again in a hotel in Manchester, where I had been taken by strangers the next day. For all these weeks I had suffered from a nervous fever. I had been found lying in the road several miles away from the house; but how I had escaped from it to get there, I don't know.

"Upon my recovery, I asked about the fate of Judge Veigh, whom they said was well and at home. No one believed a word of my story, and who can blame them? And who can imagine my grief when, arriving at my home two months later, I learned that Judge Veigh had never been heard of since that night? I then regretted the pride, which since the first few days after the recovery had forbidden me to repeat my story and insist upon its truth.

"With all that later occurred—the examination of the house; the failure to find any room looking like the one, which I have described; the attempt to have me certified insane, and my triumph over my accusers—the readers of the newspaper are familiar. After all these years I am still confident that diggings would reveal the secret of the disappearance of my friend, and possibly of the occupants and owners of the destroyed house."

Colonel McArdle died in Frankfort on the thirteenth day of December, in the year 1879.

The Other Lodgers

"In order to take that train," said Colonel Levering, sitting in the Waldorf-Astoria hotel, "you will have to remain all night in Atlanta. That is a fine city, but I advise you not to stay at the Breathitt House, one of the hotels. It is an old wooden building in need of repairs. There are breaches in the walls that you could throw a cat through. The bedrooms have no locks on the doors, no furniture but a single chair in each, and a bed without bedding—just a mattress. But you cannot be sure that you will have these lodgings for yourself, as you might be stowed in with a lot of strangers. Sir, it is a most terrible hotel. The night that I passed in it was most uncomfortable. I got in late and was shown to my room by an apologetic night-clerk. I was worn out by two days of railway travel and had not recovered from a gunshot wound in the head, received in an argument. Rather than look for better quarters I lay down on the mattress without removing my clothing and fell asleep.

"I woke up in the middle of the night. The moon was shining in through the window, lighting up the room with a bluish light, which seemed a bit spooky.

"Imagine my surprise when I saw the floor occupied by at least a dozen other lodgers! I sat up, damning the management of that hotel, and was about to jump from the bed to go and make trouble for the night clerk — when something in the situation stopped me. I suppose I was what a story-writer might call 'frozen with terror.' For those men were all dead!

"They lay on their backs, orderly along the sides of the room, their feet to the walls. All the faces were covered, but under their white cloths the features of the two bodies that lay in the moonlight showed in sharp profile nose and chin.

"I thought it was a bad dream and tried to cry out, as one does in a nightmare, but could not make a sound. At last, with much effort I threw my feet to the floor and passed between the rows of covered faces, I escaped from the infernal place and ran to the office.

"The night-clerk was there, behind the desk — just sitting and staring. He did not rise: My entrance had no effect on him, though I must have looked like a corpse myself. It occurred to me then that I had not really observed the fellow before. He was a little chap, with a colorless face, and the whitest, blankest eyes I ever saw. He had no more expression than the back of my hand. His clothing was a dirty gray.

"'Damn you!' I said; 'what do you mean?' Just the same, I was shaking like a leaf in the wind and did not recognize my own voice.

"The night-clerk rose, bowed and—well, he was no longer there, and at that moment I felt a hand laid upon my shoulder from behind. Just imagine that if you can! Awfully frightened, I turned and saw a kind-faced gentleman, who asked:

"'What is the matter, my friend?'

"It did not take long until I told him, but before I had finished, he went pale himself. 'See here,' he said, 'are you telling the truth?'

"I had now come to my senses and terror had given place to indignation. 'If you dare to doubt it,' I said, 'I'll hammer the life out of you!'

"'No,' he replied, 'don't do that; just sit down until I tell you. This is not a hotel. It used to be; later it was a hospital. Now it is unoccupied, waiting for a new tenant. The room that you mention was the dead-room—there were always plenty of dead. The fellow that you call the night-clerk used to be that, but later he booked the patients as they were brought in. I don't understand his being here. He has been dead for a few weeks.'

"'And who are you?' I blurted out.

"'Oh, I look after the premises. I happened to be passing by just now, and seeing a light in here came in to investigate. Let us have a look into that room,' he added, lifting the candle from the desk.

"'I'll see you at the devil first!' I said, running out of the door into the street.

"Sir, that Breathitt House, in Atlanta, is a beastly place! Don't you stop there."

"God forbid! Your account of it certainly does not suggest comfort. By the way, Colonel, when did all that occur?"

"In September, 1864—shortly after the siege."

The Thing At Nolan

To the south of the road between Leesville and Hardy, in the State of Missouri, stands an abandoned house. Nobody has lived in it since the summer of 1879, and it is fast going to pieces. For some three years before the date mentioned above, it was occupied by the family of Charles May, from one of whose ancestors the creek near which it stands took its name.

Mr. May's family consisted of a wife, an adult son, and two young girls. The son's name was John—the names of the daughters are unknown to the writer of this sketch.

John May was a morose man, not easily moved to anger, but having an uncommon gift of hate. His father was quite the opposite; sunny and jovial, but with a short temper. He held no resentments, and once his anger was gone, was quick to make peace.

He had a brother living nearby who was unlike him in all of these traits, and it was a current joke in the neighborhood that John had inherited his nature from his uncle.

One day there was a misunderstanding between father and son, harsh words were exchanged, and the father hit the son in the face with his fist. John wiped away the blood, fixed his eyes upon the already sorry offender and said with cold poise, "You will die for that."

The words were overheard by two brothers named Jackson, who were approaching the men at that moment; but as they saw them engaged in a quarrel they retired. Charles May later told his wife about the incident and explained that he had apologized to the son for the blow, but without avail; the young man not only rejected his offers, but refused to withdraw his terrible threat. Nevertheless, John continued to live with the family, and things went on very much as before.

One Sunday morning in June, 1879, about two weeks after the incident, May senior left the house after breakfast, taking a spade with him. He said that he was going to dig a hole at a spring in the forest, so that the cattle could obtain water. John remained in the house for some hours, occupied with shaving himself, writing letters, and reading a newspaper. His manner was what it usually was.

At two o'clock he left the house. At five, he returned. For some reason, the time of his departure and that of his return were noted by his mother and sisters, as was attested at his trial for murder. It was observed that his clothing was wet, as if he had been removing blood-stains from it. His manner was strange, his look was wild. He complained of illness, and as he went to his room he went to bed.

May senior did not return. Later that evening the neighbors were aroused, and the following day a search was undertaken through the forest, where the spring was. Only both men's footprints in the clay around the spring were discovered. John May in the meantime had grown rapidly worse with what the local physician called brain fever, and in his confusion ranted about murder, but did not say whom he thought had been murdered, nor whom he imagined to have done the deed. But his threat was recalled by the brothers Jackson and he was arrested on suspicion.

Public opinion was strongly against him, and if it had not been for his illness he would probably have been hanged by the mob. As it was, a meeting of the neighbors was held on Tuesday and a committee was called in to watch the case.

On Wednesday everything was changed. From the town of Nolan came a story, which put quite a different light on the matter. Nolan consisted of a school house, a blacksmith's shop, a "store," and a half-dozen houses.

The store was kept by one Henry Odell, a cousin of the elder May. On the afternoon of the Sunday of May's disappearance, Mr. Odell and four of his neighbors were sitting in the store, smoking and talking. It was a warm day; and both the front and the back door were open. At about three o'clock Charles May, who was well known to three of them, entered at the front door and went out at the rear.

He did not look at them, nor return their greeting, for he was evidently seriously hurt. Above the left eyebrow was a wound—a deep gash from which the blood flowed, covering the whole left side of the face and neck and his light-gray shirt. Oddly enough, the first thought in the minds of all was that he had been in a fight and was going to the brook directly at the back of the store to wash himself.

Perhaps there was a certain backwoods politeness, which kept them from following him to offer help; the court records, from which this narrative is drawn, are silent as to anything but the facts. They waited for him to return, but he did not return.

By the brook behind the store is a forest that extends for six miles to the hills. As soon as it became known that he had been seen in Nolan, there was a marked change in public sentiment.

The watch committee went out of existence without the formality of a resolution. Search along the bottom lands of May Creek was stopped, and the entire male population of the region took to beating the bush around the area. But no trace was found of the missing man.

One of the strangest things in this case is the trial of a man for murder where the body of the victim is not found nor seen—or even known to be dead. We are all more or less familiar with the quirks of frontier law, but this instance is unique. However that may be, upon recovering from his illness, John May was indicted for the murder of his missing father. The defense did not object and the case was tried on its merits.

The prosecution was spiritless; the defense easily established—with regard to the deceased—an alibi. If during the time, in which John May must have killed Charles May, Charles May was miles away from where John May must have been, it is obvious that the deceased must have come to his death at the hands of someone else.

John May was declared innocent and immediately left the country, and has never been heard of since that day. Shortly afterward his mother and sisters moved to St. Louis.

The farm passed into the hands of a man who owns the land next to it, and has a house of his own; the May house has ever since been empty, and has the reputation of being haunted.

One day after the May family had left the country, some boys found under a mass of dead leaves, but partly exposed, a spade. It was nearly new and bright, except for a spot on one edge, which was rusted and stained with blood. The tool had the initials C. M. cut into the handle.

This discovery sparked the public excitement again. The earth near the spot, where the spade was found, was carefully examined, and they finally found the dead body of a man. It had been buried under two feet of soil and the spot was covered with a layer of dead leaves.

There was a wound above the left eyebrow—a deep gash from which blood had flowed, covering the whole left side of the face and neck and the light-gray shirt. The skull had been cut through by the blow. The body was that of Charles May.

But what was it that had walked through Mr. Odell's store at Nolan?

The Difficulty Of Crossing A Field

One morning in July, 1854, a planter named Williamson was sitting with his wife and a child on the veranda of his house. Right in front of the house was a lawn, perhaps fifty yards between the house and a public road called the "pike."

Beyond this road lay a meadow of ten acres, flat and without a tree or any object on its surface. At the time there was not even a domestic animal in the field. In another field, beyond the meadow, a dozen men were at work under an overseer.

Throwing away the stump of a cigar, the planter rose and said: "I forgot to tell Andrew about those horses." Andrew was the supervisor. Williamson strolled down the gravel walk, passed across the road and into the meadow. There he paused for a moment as he closed the gate, to greet a neighbor, Armour Wren, who lived on the next plantation. Mr. Wren was in a carriage with his son James, a boy of thirteen. When he had driven two hundred yards from the point of meeting, Mr. Wren said to his son: "I forgot to tell Mr. Williamson about those horses."

Mr. Wren had sold some horses to Mr. Williamson, which should have been sent for that day, but for some reason it would be difficult to deliver them until the next day. The coachman was told to drive back, and as the vehicle turned around, Williamson was seen by all three, walking across the meadow.

At that moment one of the coach horses stumbled and nearly fell. Just as it had recovered itself, James Wren cried: "Why, father, what has happened to Mr. Williamson?"

It is not the purpose of this narrative to answer that question. Mr. Wren's strange account of the matter, given under oath in the course of legal proceedings, follows here:

"My son's cry made me look toward the spot where I had seen the deceased [sic] a moment before, but he was not there, nor was he anywhere to be seen. I cannot say that at the moment I was startled, or realized the seriousness of the situation, but I thought it strange. My son, however, was greatly astonished and kept repeating his question until we arrived at the gate. My other boy Sam was similarly affected, but I think more by my son's manner than by anything he had himself seen. [This sentence in the testimony was stricken out.]

"As we got out of the carriage, and while Sam was hanging [sic] the team to the fence, Mrs. Williamson, with her child in her arms and followed by several servants, came running down the walk in, crying: 'He is gone, he is gone! Oh God! what an awful thing!' and many other such exclamations. I got from them the impression that they related to something more—than the mere vanishing of her husband, even if that had occurred before her eyes.

"Her manner was wild, but nothing more than was natural under the conditions. I have no reason to believe that she had lost her mind. I have never since seen nor heard of Mr. Williamson."

This testimony was verified in almost every detail by the only other eye-witness (if that is a proper term)–the boy James. Mrs. Williamson had lost her sanity and the servants were, of course, not able to testify. The boy James Wren had at first stated that he *SAW* the disappearance, but there is nothing of this in his testimony. None of the people working in the field to which Williamson was going had seen him at all, and the search of the entire plantation did not give any results. The most horrific fictions were common in that part of the State for many years, and probably to this day; but what has been here related is all that is certainly known of the matter. The courts decided that Williamson was dead, and his estate was distributed according to law.

An Unfinished Race

James Burne Worson was a shoemaker who lived in Leamington, Warwickshire, England. He had a little shop in one of the alleys. In his humble place he was considered an honest man, although like many of his kind in English towns he was addicted to drinking.

When he was drunk he would make foolish bets. On one of these occasions he was boasting of his prowess as an athlete, and the outcome was a match against nature. For a stake of one coin he was going to run all the way to Coventry and back, a distance of more than forty miles. This was on the third day of September in 1873. He set out at once, and the man with whom he had made the bet, accompanied by Barham Wise, a linen draper, and Hamerson Burns, a photographer, followed in a wagon.

For several miles, Worson went on very well without much fatigue, for he had really great powers of endurance and was not drunk enough to weaken them. The three men in the wagon kept a short distance in the back, giving him occasional friendly cheer, as the spirit moved them.

Suddenly the man seemed to stumble, sloped headlong forward, uttered a terrible cry and vanished! He did not fall to the ground—he vanished before he even touched it. No trace of him was ever discovered. After remaining at the spot for some time, the three men returned to Leamington, told their astonishing story and were then taken into custody. But they were of good standing, had always been considered truthful, and were sober at the time of the incident.

Nothing ever emerged to question their account of the strange adventure. The public opinion on its truth, however, was divided throughout the United Kingdom. If they had something to hide, their choice of means is certainly one of the most amazing ever made by sane human beings.

Charles Ashmore's Trail

The family of Christian Ashmore consisted of his wife, his mother, two grown daughters, and a son of sixteen years. They lived in Troy, New York, were well-off and respectable persons, and had many friends. In 1871 they moved from Troy to Richmond, Indiana, and a year later to the vicinity of Quincy, Illinois, where Mr. Ashmore bought a farm and lived on it. At a distance from the farmhouse was a spring with a flow of clear, cold water, where the family derived its supply for use at all seasons.

On the evening of the ninth of November in 1878, at about nine o'clock, young Charles Ashmore left the family circle around the hearth, took a bucket and went toward the spring. When he did not return, the family became uneasy, and going to the door by which he had left the house, his father called his name, but did not receive an answer. He then took a lantern, and with the eldest daughter, Martha, went out to search. A light snow had fallen and covered the path, but the young man's trail was visible; each footprint was clearly defined. After walking more than half-way, the father stopped, and raising his lantern stood looking into the darkness ahead.

"What is the matter, father?" the girl asked. This was the matter: the trail of the young man had abruptly ended, and all beyond was unbroken snow. The last footprints were as clear as any in the line. Mr. Ashmore looked upward. The stars were shining; there was not a cloud in the sky. Walking wide around the last tracks, so as to leave them undisturbed for further examination, the man proceeded to the spring and the girl followed. Neither had spoken a word of what both had seen. The spring was covered with ice, hours old.

As they returned to the house, they noted the snow on both sides of the trail. No tracks led away from it. The morning light showed nothing more. Smooth, spotless, the shallow snow was everywhere.

Four days later, the grief-stricken mother herself went to the spring for water. She came back and told that as she had passed the spot where the footprints had ended, she had heard the voice of her son and had eagerly called to him.

Wandering around the place, she thought the voice to come from one direction, then from another, until she was too exhausted to go on. When she was asked what the voice had said, she was unable to tell, but stated that the words were perfectly clear.

In a moment the entire family was at the place, but nothing was heard, and the voice was believed to be a hallucination caused by the mother's great anxiety.

But for months afterward, the voice was heard by several other people too. All said that it was the voice of Charles Ashmore, and all agreed that it came from a great distance, loud and clear. But no one could tell from what direction, nor could they repeat its words. The silence in between grew longer and longer, the voice fainter and farther, and by midsummer it was heard no more.

If anybody knows the fate of Charles Ashmore, it is probably his mother. She is dead.

A Note On The Text

The stories in this edition are based on the original publications, and have been revised to accommodate a modern readership. Care has been taken to deliver them in a way that is both easy to read and a joy to behold, without losing their distinct character.

Just as a Medieval painter lets us see a picture without us taking notice of its brushstrokes, it is our aim to let you read a story without being deterred by its style.

Good writing derives its quality not from form, but from substance. It can be reworded, translated, and abridged, and still be the same; just as the foundation of literature, mythology, has been able to pass through millennia of variations, and still retain its essential core. Or, to mention a more recent example, the fairy-tales transcribed by the Brothers Grimm, whose timeless quality stand in direct relation to the crystal clear diction. Since times immemorial has Cinderella's lost shoe felt more feet than a sidewalk, and still finds the right foot in the end.

While the flowery language of a bygone era holds a historical lure, it at the same time acts as an anchor, whose ship is submerged in the rising tide of time.

The way it was written chains it to its own era, locked in a cell, where its overwrought words and embellished clauses collect cobwebs and dust.

The actual meaning often falls victim to the manner. Style has been more a burden than an asset the past 400 years, and has marred literature to such an extent that many classics are almost impossible to read.

The over-decoration of sentences with empty adjectives, adverbs and nouns often only leaves the outlines of its creations discernible in a black sea of words that have long since gone out of fashion. One can tell the monster from the ghoul, but not the meaning from the word.

Many of the creations, such as Lovecraft's Cthulhu Mythos or Shelley's Frankenstein's Monster, have long since surpassed their literary origin and moved into the realm of modern folklore.

More people know of Lovecraft's creatures than have read his stories, just as Frankenstein's Monster was made popular not by the written word, but by the motion picture. It is time to change his circumstance and let the words speak with a new clarity.

Let us view the painting, as we leave the brushstrokes to the artist, and rejoice at classic storytelling finally unobscured by style.

A CATALOG OF SELECTED
ARK TUNDRA
BOOKS

H. P. Lovecraft

Lovecraft: Easy To Read

ISBN: 978-91-88895-00-4
104pp, 5 x 8.

Contains *Dagon, The Horror At Red Hook*, and other classic tales--completely revised and abridged.
An outstanding addition to every collection!

Easy To Read Series Vol. 1

E. A. Poe

Poe: Easy To Read

ISBN: 978-91-88895-02-8
118pp. 5 x 8.

Contains five completely revised and abridged stories from the undisputed master of romantic horror!

Easy To Read Series Vol. 2

Visit our publishing site for information
on new exciting titles!

imprint.arktundra.com

www.ingramcontent.com/pod-product-compliance
Lightning Source LLC
Chambersburg PA
CBHW022037170626
46808CB00003B/1251